Stan the Dog Becomes Superdog

written and illustrated
by Scoular Anderson

PICTURE WINDOW BOOKS
Minneapolis, Minnesota

Editor: Nick Healy
Page Production: Melissa Kes
Art Director: Nathan Gassman
Associate Managing Editor: Christianne Jones

First American edition published in 2007 by
Picture Window Books
5115 Excelsior Boulevard
Suite 232
Minneapolis, MN 55416
877-845-8392
www.picturewindowbooks.com

First published in 2006 by A&C Black Publishers Limited, 38 Soho Square,
London, W1D 3HB, with the title SUPERDOG STAN.

Text and illustrations copyright © 2006 Scoular Anderson

Printed in the United States of America.

Library of Congress Cataloging-in-Publication Data
Anderson, Scoular.
Stan the dog becomes superdog / written and illustrated by Scoular Anderson.
p. cm. — (Read-it! chapter books)
Summary: While out on his "walks" Stan the dog learns how to overcome many
obstacles and when he shows up at the local dog show, he is able to display his new
talents.
ISBN-13: 978-1-4048-3131-5 (library binding)
ISBN-10: 1-4048-3131-2 (library binding)
[1. Dogs—Fiction. 2. Walking—Fiction. 3. Contests—Fiction. 4. Dog shows—Fiction.]
I. Title.
PZ7.A5495Stu 2006
[Fic]—dc22   2006027274

Table of Contents

Chapter One

Stan's family was
having breakfast.

Food was one of Stan's favorite things.
If he stayed nearby, Stan knew he might
get some, too.

The person Stan called Crumble always dropped crumbs on the floor.

The person Stan called Handout always gave him a handout.

Stan got a special surprise when the person he called Big Belly dropped a cereal box on the floor.

The one Stan called Can Opener was very angry. She was the one who usually prepared Stan's meals.

Can Opener chased Stan into his bed.

Stan lay down and heaved a big sigh.
He heard Can Opener and Big Belly talking
about him.

A little later, Stan heard Handout and Crumble talking about him.

Stan listened to Can Opener's plan.

Chapter Two

Big Belly and Stan
set out on their
walk. They went
along the path
near the river.

> I like the river path.
> There are lots of
> interesting smells.

After a bit, Big Belly
stopped. He took a
blanket out of his bag.

Big Belly made himself comfy on the bank of the river.

Then he took something else out of his bag.

Big Belly threw the ball, and Stan went bounding after it. He was back in a flash.

Big Belly threw the ball again ... and again ... and again.

Stan enjoyed himself, unlike Big Belly.

Stan ran up and down the river path for a long time.

At last, he noticed a drainpipe.

The field was full of piles of hay, but there was no sign of the ball.

Sniff! Sniff!

Stan sniffed every pile until he finally found it.

By the time he got back to the river, Big Belly had packed up and was ready to go home.

Chapter Three

In the afternoon, it was Handout's turn to take Stan for a walk. Handout planned to meet his pal Emmo at the corner. Stan and Handout waited there for a long time.

At last, Handout jumped off the wall.

They went to the park, where they found Emmo playing soccer.

The boys began to play, and Stan tried to join in.

Stan had to sit and watch.

Stan ran back toward the street.

Stan picked up the jacket and headed back toward the park.

But then he realized he was stuck outside the park wall.

Stan saw Scott and Sprinter heading toward him.

There was a plank lying at the edge of an empty lot.

But the wobbly plank was lying on a barrel. When Stan ran across, the plank tipped.

Stan slid and landed face-first in a muddy puddle just as Sprinter passed by.

Stan tried another escape
route. He found a wall
that was low enough
to climb over.

He climbed
up a shed roof
and down the
other side.

But he got stuck on his way down.

Stan arrived back at the soccer fields just as Handout and Emmo were saying goodbye. Handout didn't even notice that Stan had been away.

Chapter Four

The next morning, Can Opener opened a can and gave Stan his breakfast.

Huh! I'm sure there is less food here than there was yesterday.

Can Opener and Crumble took Stan to the park after he had eaten.

She doesn't take any nonsense. I'll get a decent walk now.

They walked along the busy main street
and stopped at the new crosswalk.

They crossed when the green
light came on.

At the park, they headed for the pond,
where Can Opener tied Stan to a bench.

Then Can Opener took Crumble to feed
the ducks.

The wind caught Crumble's empty bag and blew it out of her hand. It landed near Stan.

He pulled on the leash so hard that the knot came undone. He chased the bag as it floated away again.

Stan caught up with the bag and licked
a few crumbs from the inside. Can Opener
scolded him when she finally caught up.

To make matters worse, Sprinter had
watched the whole event.

It was a bad end to another bad walk.

Chapter Five

The next day, one of Can Opener's friends stopped by to visit.

Stan called the lady Friendly. She was a dog trainer, but she always spoke kindly to him. Also, Stan knew she kept dog biscuits in her pocket.

Can Opener appeared with the coffee, and they sat down on the sofa.

35

When she had finished her coffee, Friendly said goodbye.

Stan ran into the living room. He jumped up on the sofa to watch Friendly go down the street.

36

Chapter Six

Later that day, the family got ready to go to the dog show. Stan stood by the door, ready to go along.

The family walked out, and the front door slammed shut.

Stan knew just what to do. He pushed open a door and went down into the basement.

He squeezed past boxes, bicycles, paint cans, old junk, and broken toys.

Stan pushed his nose against a little door.

With a creak, the door opened, and he climbed out into the yard.

Stan ran around the side of the house and through the front gate, sniffing as he went.

He ran down the street—sniff, sniff, sniffing his way.

Soon Stan realized he wasn't the only dog on the street. There were other dogs all over the place!

All of the dogs and their owners were heading for a huge building. Stan followed them through the door.

As Stan was squeezing through the crowd, he caught sight of Sprinter.

Stan pushed onward.

Stan ran forward, sniffing. He ran through a tube lying on the ground.

He jumped over a wall and then climbed up and down a steep slope.

He ran along a wobbly piece of wood.

He came to a place where handkerchiefs lay scattered on the ground. He could still smell Friendly's scent.

Then he noticed something else that was familiar.

As soon as Stan pressed the button, a
light came on, and there was a huge roar of
clapping and cheering.

STORKSTON ANNUAL DOG SHOW
EVENT
27
OBSTACLE RACE
FOR THE STORKSTON SUPERDOG CUP

Stan saw his family standing nearby. They all looked very puzzled. Then he caught sight of Friendly, too.

After that, the whole crowd wanted to meet Superdog Stan.

Can Opener took a scarf from her pocket to use as a leash. Then Stan led his family home at great speed.

Look for More *Read-it!* Chapter Books

The Badcat Gang
Beastly Basil
Cat Baby
Cleaner Genie
Clever Monkeys
Contest Crazy
Disgusting Denzil
Duperball
Elvis the Squirrel
Eric's Talking Ears
High Five Hank
Hot Dog and the Talent Competition
Nelly the Monstersitter
On the Ghost Trail
Scratch and Sniff
Sid and Bolter
The Thing in the Basement
Tough Ronald

Looking for a specific title? A complete list
of *Read-it!* Chapter Books is available on our Web site:
www.picturewindowbooks.com